Rosie's Cafe

Rosie's Cafe

Darryl De Carteret Pochin

Published by Darryl De Carteret Pochin, 2024.

ROSIE'S CAFE

First edition. December 14, 2024.

ISBN: 979-8230792079

Written by Darryl De Carteret Pochin.

Rosie's
Cafe

By
Darryl De Carteret-Pochin

Prologue

The cottage was quiet, save for the faint ticking of the clock on the mantle. Rosie Miller sat alone at her kitchen table, a cup of tea growing cold in her hands. Outside, the late afternoon sun cast long shadows over the garden, but Rosie barely noticed. Her gaze was fixed on the photograph resting in front of her, a picture of her and Tom on their thirtieth wedding anniversary.

She traced the edges of the frame with her finger, her heart heavy. It had been two years since Tom's passing, but some days it felt like yesterday. She missed his laugh, the way he hummed when he read the paper, the steady presence he'd brought to her life. Without him, the house felt too big, the days too long.

Her children, Emily and Peter, had been her lifeline, encouraging her to stay busy and reminding her that life still had meaning. And the florist shop where she worked had been a refuge of sorts, a place where she could lose herself in the simple joy of arranging flowers. But even there, a dull ache followed her, a quiet reminder of all she had lost.

She sighed, setting her tea aside and rising to her feet. She had once been full of dreams, the kind of woman who found joy in life's smallest moments. Now, she felt like a shadow of herself, drifting through the days without direction.

Rosie glanced out the window, her gaze lingering on the horizon where the sky met the sea. Somewhere out there, she thought, was a version of her life she hadn't yet discovered. She didn't know it yet, but the letter waiting in her mailbox that very evening would change everything.

It would lead her to a seaside café, a forgotten part of her family's legacy, and a second chance at joy. It would challenge her to confront her grief, rediscover her passions, and open her heart to new possibilities.

Rosie turned away from the window, her thoughts elsewhere. For now, she was still a widow sitting in a quiet kitchen, unaware that her life was about to take a turn she could never have imagined.

Chapter 1
A Quiet Morning at the Florist Shop

Rosie Miller hummed quietly to herself as she snipped the stems of fresh tulips, arranging them into a cheerful bouquet. The faint scent of roses and lilies lingered in the air, mingling with the earthy undertone of potting soil. The florist shop, tucked neatly on the corner of Main Street, had been her refuge for years, a place of simple beauty and steady routine.

"Rosie, that's a masterpiece," Janet's voice floated over from behind the counter. Janet, the owner of the shop and Rosie's long-time friend, had a way of making even the simplest arrangements feel like art.

"Oh, stop it," Rosie replied, smiling. "It's just a little sunshine in a vase." She tied a yellow ribbon around the bouquet and placed it gently in the display.

The shop bell jingled as a young couple walked in, hand in hand. Rosie greeted them warmly, helping them choose a bouquet for their anniversary. Moments like these, helping people celebrate life's little joys, reminded her why she loved her work.

BUT AS THE COUPLE LEFT, hand in hand, a pang of loneliness settled in her chest. It had been two years since Tom, her husband of thirty-five years, passed away. Some days, the loss felt like a dull ache; on others, it was a sharp, unbearable void.

"Rosie, love, you've got that look again," Janet said gently, interrupting her thoughts.

Rosie sighed. "I'm fine, really. Just thinking about Tom."

Janet nodded. "He'd want you to be happy, you know."

"I know," Rosie said softly.

The day passed uneventfully and Rosie returned home to her cozy cottage, where she was greeted by Tiggy, her cat, who purred at her touch, waiting for some food. Tiggy was a constant in Rosie's life, a small bundle of warmth and comfort wrapped in soft, fluffy fur. She had been a part of the family for over ten years, a rescue cat with wide green eyes and a coat the colour of autumn leaves and storm clouds, browny-grey with streaks of tawny and cream. She was friendly to everyone, but it was clear to anyone who met her that Tiggy's heart belonged to Rosie.

Rosie often joked that Tiggy had chosen her, not the other way around. It had been a rainy afternoon when Emily had convinced her to visit the local animal shelter. Rosie had still been deep in grief after losing Tom, hesitant to bring a pet into her life. But when Tiggy had padded over, rubbing against Rosie's leg and letting out a soft, trilling purr, something inside her had shifted.

"She's the one," Emily had said with a grin, and Rosie couldn't argue.

Introduction to Rosie's Life

THE SHOP BELL TINKLED gently as Rosie unlocked the door to *Janet's Flowers & Gifts*. A crisp spring breeze followed her inside, carrying with it the scent of blooming daffodils and fresh rain. It was early yet, the street outside still sleepy and quiet, but Rosie loved these moments. They gave her time to prepare the shop before the day's activity began.

She shrugged off her coat, hung it neatly on the peg behind the counter, and tied her apron around her waist. The familiar motions were comforting, like slipping into a well-worn pair of slippers. The shop itself was small but charming, with wooden shelves lined with pots of succulents, shelves filled with glass vases, and cheerful displays of cut flowers in every colour imaginable.

Rosie paused to adjust a cluster of gerberas that had shifted overnight. "There you are," she murmured, stepping back to admire their symmetry. She loved the work, not just the creativity of arranging flowers but the way they could brighten someone's day. In this town, flowers meant celebration, comfort, and connection.

As she worked, the door swung open, and Janet bustled in, carrying two cups of coffee and a pastry bag.

"Good morning, Rosie!" Janet chirped, her auburn hair peeking out from beneath a knitted beret.

"Morning, Janet," Rosie replied with a smile. She took the offered coffee gratefully. "You're a lifesaver."

Janet laughed. "I know how you get before your first cup." She set the pastry bag on the counter. "And don't forget the almond croissant. Fresh from the bakery!"

Rosie chuckled. "You spoil me."

"That's what friends are for," Janet said with a wink. "Besides, you're the heart of this place. I'd be lost without you."

It was true that Rosie had become indispensable to the shop over the years. Her arrangements were renowned throughout the town, and her gentle manner drew in loyal customers who valued her attention to detail. Janet often joked that Rosie could turn weeds into wedding bouquets.

The two women worked side by side, chatting as they stocked the front displays and prepared for the day. The rhythm of their friendship was comfortable and unspoken, built on years of trust.

"Got any plans this weekend?" Janet asked as she unwrapped a delivery of fresh roses.

Rosie hesitated. "Emily's coming over for dinner on Sunday," she said. "Peter might stop by too if he's not too busy with work."

Janet nodded, giving her a knowing look. "They worry about you, you know."

"I know," Rosie admitted. "They mean well, but I wish they'd stop fussing. I'm fine, really."

Janet raised an eyebrow but said nothing. She had known Rosie long enough to recognised when she was deflecting.

<u>Rosie's Family</u>

EMILY ARRIVED LATER that evening, as she often did on Sundays. Rosie had prepared a simple roast chicken dinner, the kind of meal Tom used to love. The table was set neatly, with her mother's old china and a vase of tulips as the centrepiece.

"Smells amazing in here," Emily said as she stepped inside, shrugging off her coat. At 32, Emily was the spitting image of her father, with his dark hair and warm brown eyes. She worked as a teacher at the local primary school, and her gentle nature mirrored Rosie's in many ways.

"Thanks, love," Rosie said, kissing her daughter's cheek. "Peter said he's stuck at the office, so it's just us tonight."

Emily sighed. "He works too much."

Rosie nodded but said nothing. Peter, her eldest, was a successful architect in the city, but his demanding job often kept him away. She missed him, though she would never admit it.

Over dinner, Emily asked about the shop, and Rosie recounted her day with a smile. But as the conversation turned to more personal matters, Emily grew serious.

"Have you thought any more about the idea of a trip?" she asked.

Rosie frowned. "What trip?"

"The one we talked about last month," Emily said patiently. "A weekend away. Somewhere nice. I think it would do you good."

"I appreciate the thought, Emily, but I'm fine where I am," Rosie replied, keeping her tone light.

Emily sighed, her frustration bubbling to the surface. "Mum, you've been saying you're 'fine' for two years. I know you miss Dad, I do too, but you deserve more than just getting by. You need something to look forward to."

Rosie's heart ached at the concern in her daughter's eyes. Emily meant well, but she couldn't understand. Losing Tom had left a void that couldn't be filled by a weekend getaway or a new hobby. Still, she hated worrying her children.

"I'll think about it," she said softly, hoping to end the discussion.

Emily gave her a long look but didn't push further.

Peter's Concern

Peter called the following evening, his deep voice crackling slightly over the line.

"Hey, Mum. How's it going?"

"Hi, love. I'm fine. Busy at the shop, as usual," Rosie replied, cradling the phone against her shoulder as she washed the dishes.

"Emily said you had dinner together yesterday," Peter said. "She mentioned...well, she's worried about you."

Rosie sighed. "You two really need to stop talking about me like I'm some fragile thing."

"We're not, Mum," Peter said gently. "We just want to make sure you're okay. You've always been the one holding everything together, and now it feels like you're...stuck."

Rosie dried her hands and sat down at the kitchen table. "It's not that simple, Peter. Losing your dad...it's not something you just move on from."

"I know," Peter said. "But maybe it's time to think about what *you* want now. You've spent so much of your life taking care of everyone else."

Rosie's throat tightened. She appreciated her children's concern, but she wasn't sure what she wanted anymore. The routines of her life, the shop, her cozy home, her quiet evenings, were comforting. But she couldn't deny that they were also a little lonely.

"I'll be fine," she said at last. "You don't need to worry about me."

Peter hesitated. "Alright, Mum. But if you ever need anything, anything at all, you know I'm just a call away."

"I know," Rosie said softly.

As the call ended, Rosie sat in silence, her thoughts swirling. Her children were right, she had spent so much of her life caring for others, from raising Emily and Peter to supporting Tom through his illness. Now, with Tom gone and her children grown, she felt unmoored, like a ship drifting without a destination.

At home, Tiggy was a lively, reassuring presence, filling the empty spaces with her quiet companionship. She had a way of knowing when Rosie needed comfort, curling up on her lap or resting her head on Rosie's hand when tears threatened to fall.

Tiggy was also a creature of routine, something Rosie found comforting. Every morning, she would wake Rosie with a gentle paw on her cheek, her purrs rumbling like a tiny motor. Breakfast time was Tiggy's favourite part of the day, and she would circle Rosie's feet as if to remind her not to forget the most important meal.

The two had developed a quiet rhythm together. Tiggy would often perch on the windowsill, her fluffy tail twitching as she watched the world outside, while Rosie sat nearby with a book or her knitting. In the evenings, Tiggy would follow Rosie from room to room, a shadow that never left her side.

A New Day

THE NEXT MORNING, ROSIE arrived at the shop early, eager to lose herself in her work. Janet greeted her with a warm smile, and the two women settled into their familiar routine.

But as Rosie arranged a bouquet of peonies for a customer, a strange thought crossed her mind. *What if Emily and Peter are right? What if there's more to life waiting for me, and I'm just too afraid to see it?*

She shook her head, brushing the thought aside. Life was fine as it was, quiet, steady, predictable.

And yet, a small part of her wondered: *What if?*

The Letter That Changes Everything

Rosie was tidying up the small but neatly kept front garden of her cottage when she noticed the envelope sitting on the doormat. It was thicker than the usual post, no grocery store flyers or bank statements today and it bore the return address of a solicitor's office she didn't recognised.

She frowned, wiping her hands on her apron before picking it up. The envelope was heavy in her hands, its cream-coloured surface pristine except for her name and address written in a precise, formal script.

Rosie glanced at the sender's address again: *Harrington & Sons Solicitors, St. Ives.*

Her heart gave a small flutter. St. Ives was a seaside town she hadn't thought about in years, not since her childhood visits to see her Aunt May.

Curiosity overcame her hesitation, and she opened the envelope, pulling out several neatly folded sheets of paper. As her eyes scanned the first page, her breath caught in her throat.

"Dear Mrs. Miller,

We are writing to inform you that you have been named the sole beneficiary of the estate of the late Miss May Evans…"

Rosie sank into her armchair, gripping the letter as though it might vanish if she let go. Aunt May, her eccentric, free-spirited aunt who had lived her life surrounded by art, music, and the sea. Rosie hadn't seen her in years, not since a strained family disagreement had created distance between May and Rosie's parents.

Her hands trembled slightly as she continued to read. Aunt May had left her everything: a seaside café called *May's Haven*, two flats located above the café, and a modest sum of money. The solicitor had provided an inventory of the property and instructions for Rosie to contact their office to arrange a visit.

She set the letter down on the side table, her thoughts spinning. Aunt May had always been a larger-than-life figure in Rosie's childhood, a woman who had lived unapologetically on her own terms.

Rosie had admired her fiercely as a little girl, sneaking glimpses of May's paintings and listening in awe to her stories about the café.

But why now? Why her?

Rosie leaned back in her chair, staring at the ceiling. The letter felt surreal, like something out of a dream.

That evening, Rosie pulled out an old photo album from the bookshelf. It was dusty from disuse, but when she opened it, memories spilled out like sunlight. There were pictures of her as a child, grinning with a missing tooth, standing next to Aunt May on the beach. May had always been striking, her auburn hair wild in the wind, her bright green eyes filled with mischief.

Rosie remembered the way May's house had smelled of salt and paint, the kitchen table always cluttered with half-finished sketches and seashells. She'd never been afraid to speak her mind, and her laugh had been loud and infectious.

But as Rosie grew older, life had gotten in the way. Visits to St. Ives became infrequent, and eventually, they stopped altogether. May had sent the occasional postcard, but even those had dwindled over the years. Rosie felt a pang of guilt now, thinking about how easily they'd lost touch.

And yet, May had thought of her in the end.

The next morning, Rosie called Emily.

"Mum, are you okay? You sound a little...distracted," Emily said after a few minutes of pleasantries.

"I'm fine, love. Just...something unexpected happened," Rosie replied.

"Unexpected?"

"I received a letter yesterday. From a solicitor." Rosie hesitated, unsure how to frame the news. "It seems Aunt May left me her estate. A café, of all things."

There was a stunned silence on the other end of the line before Emily finally said, "A café? Aunt May left you a café?"

"Yes, and two flats above it. And a bit of money too. I don't even know where to begin."

"Well, first of all, congratulations, Mum!" Emily said, her voice brightening. "This could be a good thing, you know. A fresh start."

"A fresh start," Rosie repeated, unsure.

"You've been stuck in one place for too long," Emily said gently. "Maybe this is a sign, Mum. You should go and see it. Who knows? You might fall in love with the place."

Rosie wasn't sure how she felt about that. She didn't know what she would find in St. Ives after all these years, and the thought of taking on something as overwhelming as a café felt impossible.

"Maybe," she said finally, more to humour her daughter than anything else.

"I'll come with you," Emily offered. "We'll make a weekend of it. It could be fun."

Rosie smiled at her daughter's enthusiasm. Emily had always been the optimistic one in the family, finding the silver lining no matter the circumstances.

"Alright," Rosie said. "Let me call the solicitor and arrange a visit."

Making Arrangements

ROSIE SPENT THE NEXT few days in a whirlwind of phone calls and planning. The solicitor, a polite man named Mr. Harrington, assured her that the café and flats were in good condition but had been unoccupied for the past year.

"It's a charming property, Mrs. Miller," he said over the phone. "Your aunt was very proud of it. I think you'll find it has great potential."

Potential. The word both intrigued and intimidated her.

Emily arranged time off work, and before Rosie knew it, they were packing a small suitcase for the weekend trip. As she zipped up the bag, she found herself wondering what Aunt May would say if she could see her now.

"You always wanted an adventure, Rosie," she imagined her aunt saying with a wink.

But was she really ready for one?

The train ride to St. Ives was a mix of nostalgia and nervous anticipation. As the countryside rolled by, Rosie found herself remembering the summers she'd spent there as a child, building sandcastles on the beach, eating ice cream on the pier, and watching Aunt May paint the sea.

Emily, sitting across from her, was busy scrolling through her phone. "Did you know St. Ives is famous for its art scene? There's even a Tate Gallery there now."

Rosie nodded absently, her thoughts elsewhere. She couldn't shake the feeling that this trip would be a turning point, though she wasn't sure how.

When they finally arrived, the town was just as she remembered, quaint and picturesque, with narrow cobbled streets, whitewashed cottages, and the smell of salt in the air. The sea sparkled in the distance, its waves crashing gently against the shore.

Emily grabbed her arm, her excitement contagious. "Come on, Mum. Let's go see your café!"

When they reached the property, Rosie stopped in her tracks. The café, painted a cheerful shade of blue, stood on a corner overlooking the harbour. It was charming in a slightly worn way, with peeling paint and a sign that read *May's Haven* hanging above the door.

"It's adorable," Emily said, snapping a photo.

Rosie stepped closer, her heart pounding. The windows were dusty, and the flower boxes beneath them were empty, but she could see the potential Mr. Harrington had mentioned.

The solicitor was waiting for them inside. He gave Rosie a firm handshake and began the tour. The café itself was small but cozy, with wooden tables, a counter, and a kitchen in the back. The flats above were modest but had stunning views of the sea.

"This is it," Rosie murmured, running her hand along the counter. She could almost imagine the place bustling with life, the smell of coffee and pastries filling the air.

"It's got charm," Emily said encouragingly.

Rosie nodded, though she wasn't sure what she was feeling. Excitement? Overwhelm? A strange sense of connection?

As she stood in the empty café, the possibilities began to take shape in her mind. Maybe this wasn't just an inheritance. Maybe it was an opportunity, a chance to start again.

Rosie sat at her kitchen table, the solicitor's letter spread out before her like a puzzle waiting to be solved. She'd already read it three times, but the words still felt surreal. Aunt May, wild, bohemian, fiercely independent Aunt May, had left her everything.

As she stared at the letter, a part of her wondered whether it was a mistake. Why her? She hadn't seen May in decades, and yet here she was, inheriting a seaside café and two flats above it. The thought was as thrilling as it was overwhelming.

A knock at the door pulled her from her thoughts. Rosie glanced at the clock, Emily was right on time, as always.

"Come in, love!" Rosie called, standing to greet her daughter.

Emily stepped inside, her arms full of a bottle of wine and a box of pastries from the local bakery. "Thought we'd have a little treat with dinner," she said, kissing her mother on the cheek. "You look a bit...distracted, Mum. Everything alright?"

Rosie hesitated, unsure how to begin. "I have some news," she said, gesturing for Emily to sit at the table.

Emily raised an eyebrow, curiosity sparking in her warm brown eyes. "What kind of news?"

Rosie slid the letter across the table, watching as her daughter picked it up and began to read.

Emily's Reaction

FOR A MOMENT, EMILY said nothing, her eyes scanning the page intently. Then she let out a low whistle.

"A café? And flats? Aunt May left you all this?"

"Apparently," Rosie said, her tone still edged with disbelief.

Emily set the letter down and looked at her mother, her expression a mixture of surprise and excitement. "Wow. I mean...wow. Did you know she was going to leave you anything?"

"No," Rosie admitted. "I hadn't heard from her in years. The last time I saw her was...oh, it must have been when you and Peter were children. She sent postcards now and then, but we drifted apart."

Emily leaned back in her chair, crossing her arms. "It's a lot to take in. What are you going to do?"

Rosie sighed. "I don't know. Part of me thinks I should just sell it all, let someone else deal with the café. But another part of me..." She trailed off, struggling to put her feelings into words.

"Another part of you what?" Emily prompted gently.

"Another part of me wonders if this could be...something. A fresh start, maybe."

Emily smiled. "I think it could be, Mum. You've spent so long in one place, stuck in the same routine. Maybe this is Aunt May's way of giving you a nudge."

They sat in silence for a moment before Emily spoke again. "Tell me about her," she said. "I don't remember much about Aunt May, just bits and pieces."

Rosie smiled faintly, her mind drifting back to her childhood. "She was...unlike anyone else in the family. Where your grandparents were practical and sensible, May was all passion and creativity. She painted, sculpted, played the piano, she even wrote poetry for a time. She wasn't interested in settling down or following the rules."

"She sounds amazing," Emily said.

"She was," Rosie agreed. "But she could also be stubborn and impulsive. She didn't always get along with my parents, they thought she was reckless, living out there on her own by the sea. But I adored her. Every summer, she'd let me stay with her for a few weeks. It was like stepping into another world. Her house was full of music and colour, and she let me run wild on the beach."

Emily leaned forward, captivated. "What happened? Why did you stop seeing her?"

Rosie hesitated, a flicker of regret passing over her face. "Life, I suppose. Your grandparents had a falling out with her over some family matter, I don't even remember the details. And when I married your dad, we were so busy with work and raising you and Peter. The years just slipped by."

Emily nodded, her gaze thoughtful. "But she never stopped thinking about you. She left all this to you, Mum. That has to mean something."

Rosie felt a lump rise in her throat. "I suppose it does," she said quietly.

Emily reached across the table, placing her hand over her mother's. "Mum, I think you should go and see it. Just take a look. What's the harm?"

Rosie bit her lip. "What if it's too much for me? I don't know anything about running a café. And it's been so long since I've been to St. Ives, I'm not even sure I'd feel at home there anymore."

Emily squeezed her hand. "You don't have to make any decisions right away. Just go and see it. If it's not right for you, you can sell it. But at least give yourself the chance to see what's possible."

Rosie hesitated, torn between her fear of the unknown and a growing spark of curiosity. Emily was right, what was the harm in looking?

"I suppose it wouldn't hurt to take a peek," she said finally.

Emily beamed. "That's the spirit! I'll come with you. We'll make a weekend of it."

"You'd do that?" Rosie asked, touched.

"Of course. I'd love to see it, and it'll be nice to spend some time with you."

Rosie smiled, the weight of the decision lifting slightly. With Emily by her side, the idea of visiting St. Ives felt less daunting.

Planning the Trip

OVER THE NEXT HOUR, they began to make plans. Emily pulled out her phone to look up train schedules, while Rosie jotted down a list of things they might need for the trip.

"Do you think the flats are furnished?" Emily asked.

"I have no idea," Rosie admitted. "The solicitor didn't say much about the state of the property, just that it's been unoccupied for about a year."

Emily grinned. "Well, if it's a bit run-down, that just adds to the adventure."

Rosie laughed, her daughter's enthusiasm infectious. For the first time since receiving the letter, she felt a glimmer of excitement. Maybe this wasn't just an overwhelming responsibility. Maybe it was an opportunity, a chance to step outside her comfort zone and rediscover a part of herself she'd forgotten.

As they finished their planning, Rosie felt a wave of gratitude for Emily. Her daughter's encouragement had turned what felt like an impossible challenge into something almost...fun.

"Thank you, love," she said as they cleared the table.

"For what?"

"For always believing in me," Rosie said softly.

Emily hugged her, her smile warm and reassuring. "Always, Mum. You're stronger than you think. And who knows? This could be the start of something amazing."

That night, as Rosie lay in bed, her mind was alive with memories of Aunt May and the possibilities that awaited her in St. Ives. She pictured the café, its windows glowing with warm light, and the sound of waves crashing just beyond the door.

A part of her was still terrified of the unknown, but another part, the part that remembered Aunt May's adventurous spirit, felt ready to take the first step.

For the first time in a long time, Rosie fell asleep with a sense of anticipation buzzing in her chest.

The train rattled gently as it sped toward the coast, its rhythmic hum matching the nervous excitement in Rosie's chest. Seated beside her, Emily stared out the window, her eyes wide with curiosity as fields and hills rolled past, giving way to the glinting blue expanse of the sea in the distance.

"We're almost there," Emily said, nudging her mother gently. "Look, Mum, the water!"

Rosie smiled, though her fingers tightened slightly on the strap of her handbag. It had been years since she'd been to St. Ives, and the mix of nostalgia and apprehension bubbling within her was almost overwhelming.

"Still as beautiful as I remember," she murmured.

The train slowed as it approached the station, and the view of the harbour came into full focus. Boats bobbed lazily in the sparkling water, and rows of whitewashed cottages lined the hills, their roofs glowing orange in the late afternoon sun. The sight was so familiar yet so distant, like a faded photograph brought back to life.

As the train pulled into the station, Emily grabbed their small suitcase and gave Rosie an encouraging smile. "Ready?"

Rosie took a deep breath. "Let's find out."

First Impressions of St. Ives

THE TOWN WAS JUST AS charming as Rosie remembered. Narrow cobblestone streets wound through clusters of art galleries, cozy cafés, and tiny shops selling seashell trinkets and handmade jewellery. The salty tang of the sea filled the air, mingling with the tempting aroma of fish and chips from a nearby stall.

"It's gorgeous," Emily said, taking in the scene. "I can see why Aunt May loved it here."

Rosie nodded, her steps slowing as she let the memories wash over her. As a child, she had run through these streets with sand between her toes, laughing as Aunt May led her on impromptu adventures.

They followed the directions from the solicitor's letter, winding through the town until they reached the harbour. There, perched on a corner with a clear view of the water, stood *May's Haven*.

The Café

May's Haven

Rosie stopped in her tracks, her breath catching. The café looked almost exactly as she remembered it, though the years had left their mark. The cheerful blue paint was faded and peeling in places, and the wooden sign hanging above the door swung slightly in the breeze, its letters weathered but still legible.

"May's Haven," Emily read aloud, a smile spreading across her face. "It's perfect."

Rosie stepped closer, her heart pounding. The large windows that faced the harbour were dusty, and the flower boxes beneath them were empty, but the building still had a sense of charm, of potential. She placed her hand on the door, which was unlocked as the solicitor had promised, and stepped inside.

The air smelled faintly of salt and wood, and the interior was quiet and dim. The café was small but cozy, with wooden tables and mismatched chairs scattered around the room. A long counter stretched along one wall, complete with an old-fashioned till and a coffee machine that looked like it hadn't been used in years.

"It's adorable," Emily said, running her fingers over the counter. "A little rough around the edges, but adorable."

Rosie nodded, her gaze sweeping the room. Despite the dust and the worn furniture, she could picture what the café might have looked like in its prime. She imagined Aunt May behind the counter, her auburn hair streaked with flour as she served coffee and pastries to a crowd of locals and tourists.

Her chest tightened with a mix of grief and gratitude. May had poured her heart into this place, and now it was Rosie's.

"What do you think?" Emily asked gently.

"I think," Rosie said slowly, "that it feels like her. Every corner of it."

Exploring the Flats

THE SOLICITOR HAD MENTIONED that the café came with two flats above it, so after a brief tour of the ground floor, Rosie and Emily climbed the narrow staircase at the back of the building.

The first flat was small and simple, with a tiny kitchen, a cozy living room, and a single bedroom. The windows overlooked the harbour, offering a stunning view of the sea. Rosie ran her fingers along the windowsill, brushing away a layer of dust.

"It needs a good cleaning," she said with a small laugh.

Emily peeked into the kitchen cupboards, inspecting the space. "I think it's charming," she said. "It just needs some love. I could see someone staying here for the summer or even living here full-time."

The second flat, located above the first, was slightly larger but just as modest. The wallpaper was faded, and the furniture looked as though it hadn't been moved in decades, but the bones of the place were solid.

"This one feels more like a home," Emily said as she wandered through the rooms. "I bet Aunt May lived here herself."

Rosie nodded, her gaze lingering on a painting hanging crookedly on the wall. It was one of May's, a bright, abstract depiction of the sea at sunset. She smiled, feeling a sudden wave of connection to her aunt.

As they made their way back down to the café, Rosie's mind was spinning. The property was far from perfect, but it was full of potential. She could see it now: the café bustling with customers, the smell of coffee and freshly baked scones filling the air, and the flats above restored to their former charm.

"It's a lot," Rosie said, sinking into one of the chairs in the café. "More than I was expecting."

Emily sat across from her, her expression thoughtful. "It is a lot," she agreed. "But I think it could be wonderful. This place has so much character and so much history."

Rosie nodded slowly. She had always thought of herself as someone who preferred the familiar, the predictable. But sitting here, in this café that had once been the heart of Aunt May's world, she felt a flicker of something she hadn't felt in years: possibility.

"It would take a lot of work to get it up and running again," she said.

"It would," Emily agreed. "But you don't have to do it alone. I could help you. And Peter too, if we twist his arm a bit."

Rosie laughed at the thought of her son, always so practical and busy, getting his hands dirty in a seaside café. "I'm not sure he'd be much use in the kitchen," she said, smiling.

Emily grinned. "We'll put him on window-cleaning duty."

They both laughed, the sound echoing softly in the empty café.

As the sun began to set, casting a warm golden light over the harbour, Rosie and Emily stood outside the café, gazing up at the building. The windows glowed faintly in the fading light, and the sound of waves crashing against the shore filled the air.

"What are you thinking, Mum?" Emily asked.

Rosie took a deep breath, letting the salty breeze fill her lungs. She had spent so much of the past two years simply surviving, going through the motions of her quiet life. But standing here, with the sea stretching out before her and Aunt May's legacy in her hands, she felt something stir within her.

"I think," she said slowly, "that I owe it to May and to myself, to at least try."

Emily beamed, throwing her arms around her mother. "That's the spirit! We'll make this place amazing, Mum. I just know it."

Rosie smiled, feeling a spark of hope ignite in her chest. It wouldn't be easy, there would be challenges and doubts and more work than she could imagine. But for the first time in a long time, she felt ready for an adventure.

And maybe, just maybe, *May's Haven* could become Rosie's haven too.

Decision to Stay for a While

THE EARLY MORNING LIGHT streamed through the window of the upstairs flat, painting the room in soft golds and blues. Rosie sat at the small kitchen table with a steaming cup of tea, staring out at the harbour. The tide was out, leaving boats tilted on their sides in the mud, waiting patiently for the water to return. It was a stillness that felt oddly reassuring, as though the town was waking up at its own unhurried pace.

Emily had gone back home the night before, needing to prepare for her workweek, but she had promised to return the following weekend to help Rosie settle in further. Now, for the first time in years, Rosie found herself completely alone.

And yet, she wasn't lonely.

The solicitor's letter lay on the table beside her, the weight of its words still sinking in. A café. Flats. Aunt May's life, handed down to her like a baton in a relay race. What was she supposed to do with it all?

Rosie's instinct had been to keep moving, to make a quick decision, sell the property and return to her comfortable routine back home. But now that she was here, the thought of leaving felt...wrong. Something about this place, this town, this café, called to her.

"I'll give it a few weeks," she said aloud, as though the sound of her voice could solidify her decision. "See how it feels. If it's not for me, I can always walk away."

The words felt safe, practical. But deep down, Rosie wondered if she already knew what her decision would be.

The first order of business was cleaning. Rosie spent the rest of the morning dusting and scrubbing the upstairs flat, determined to make it feel more like home. She opened the windows wide, letting in the fresh sea breeze, and washed the curtains to rid them of the stale, musty smell that clung to the room.

As she worked, she stumbled across little reminders of Aunt May: a stack of art books on a rickety shelf, a jar of seashells on the windowsill, and a tin box tucked into the back of a cupboard. Inside the box were handwritten recipes, some of them yellowed with age.

Rosie sat down at the table and leafed through them, her hands trembling slightly. May's familiar, looping handwriting filled the pages, accompanied by little notes in the margins:

- Add more lemon zest if it's for the Johnsons, they like it tart.
- Perfect for summer afternoons! Serve with clotted cream.

Rosie smiled, imagining her aunt bustling around the café's kitchen, humming as she baked.

Exploring the Café

ONCE THE FLAT FELT liveable, Rosie turned her attention to the café downstairs. It was in better shape than she had expected, though the dust and cobwebs suggested it hadn't seen much activity in a long time. The furniture was sturdy, if a little mismatched, and the long counter had a charming, old-fashioned feel.

The kitchen was small but functional, with an industrial oven, a battered but sturdy prep table, and a set of shelves lined with jars and utensils. Rosie found herself running her fingers over the worn surfaces, imagining what it might be like to work here, to bring the space back to life.

She made a list of things that needed attention:

• Clean and polish the windows to let in more light.

• Paint the walls to brighten the space.

• Replace the café sign outside, it was too faded to draw customers.

• Restock the kitchen with fresh ingredients.

It was a daunting list, but it also filled her with a strange sense of purpose. For the first time in a long while, she felt like she had a project, something that was hers to shape and create.

That afternoon, Rosie ventured out into the town. She needed supplies for cleaning and cooking, and she thought it might be a good idea to introduce herself to a few of the locals. After all, if she decided to reopen the café, she would need the community's support.

Her first stop was the hardware store, a cozy little shop tucked between a bakery and a bookshop. The bell above the door jingled as she entered, and a man in his sixties looked up from behind the counter.

"Afternoon," he said with a friendly nod. "What can I do for you?"

"Afternoon," Rosie replied. "I'm looking for some paint, something bright and cheerful. Yellow, maybe."

The man grinned. "Doing a bit of redecorating?"

"Something like that," Rosie said. "I'm Rosie, by the way. Rosie Miller. I just inherited May's Haven."

The man's eyes lit up with recognition. "Ah, May's niece! I thought I recognised you. I'm Charlie. My bookshop's just next door to the café."

Rosie smiled, warmed by his enthusiasm. "It's nice to meet you, Charlie. I'm still figuring out what to do with the place, but I thought a bit of cleaning and painting would be a good start."

"Good idea," Charlie said. "May's Haven's been empty for too long. Folks around here will be glad to see it brought back to life."

Rosie's chest tightened slightly at the weight of his words. There was a lot of expectation tied to the café, expectation she wasn't sure she could meet. But Charlie's encouragement felt genuine, and it gave her a small boost of confidence.

After finishing her errands, Rosie returned to the café with bags full of supplies. She spent the rest of the afternoon scrubbing the café windows until they gleamed, then set about testing a few of the recipes from Aunt May's tin.

She started with a lemon drizzle cake, following the handwritten instructions carefully. As the cake baked, the smell of citrus and sugar filled the air, blending with the salty breeze that drifted in through the open windows.

When the timer went off, Rosie pulled the cake from the oven and set it on the counter to cool. She cut herself a small slice, taking a bite as she gazed out at the harbour.

It was delicious light, tangy, and sweet.

Rosie felt a flicker of pride. Maybe she didn't know everything about running a café, but she did know how to bake. And maybe, just maybe, that was enough to start.

A Late-Night Conversation

THAT EVENING, ROSIE called Emily to share her thoughts.

"How's it going, Mum?" Emily asked. "Still feeling overwhelmed?"

"A little," Rosie admitted. "But I've decided to stay for a while. Just to see if this could be...something."

Emily's voice brightened. "That's wonderful! I knew you'd love it there."

"It's not love, exactly," Rosie said, laughing. "But it feels...right, somehow. Like I'm supposed to be here."

"I'm proud of you, Mum," Emily said warmly. "And don't forget, you're not alone in this. I'll come back this weekend to help, and I'm sure Peter will pitch in if we ask."

ROSIE SMILED, COMFORTED by her daughter's support. "Thank you, love. I couldn't do this without you."

"You can," Emily said firmly. "You're stronger than you think."

As Rosie climbed into bed that night, she felt a strange mix of exhaustion and exhilaration. The day had been long and full of work, but it had also been satisfying in a way she hadn't felt in years.

She wasn't sure where this journey would take her or what she would ultimately decide, but for now, she was willing to stay.

And that, she thought as she drifted off to sleep, was a start.

The upstairs flat quickly became Tiggy's kingdom. She spent hours exploring every nook and cranny, occasionally squeezing herself into spots too small for a cat her size. Rosie often found her napping on the windowsill, basking in the sunlight with her tail draped over the edge like a fluffy banner.

But it was the café downstairs that truly captured Tiggy's attention. Tiggy loved to curl up on one of the window seats while Rosie worked, watching customers come and go with wide, curious eyes. She was a natural at charming visitors, strolling across the floor with her plume-like tail held high and pausing just long enough to accept a scratch behind the ears or a compliment on her beautiful coat.

"She's part of the charm of this place," Margaret often said, laughing as Tiggy brushed against her legs. "You should put her on the payroll."

Rosie couldn't deny it. Tiggy had become a kind of unofficial mascot for Rosie's Café, her presence adding to the warmth and homeliness that drew people in.

Chapter 2.
Exploring the Town and Meeting the Locals

The following morning, Rosie woke to the sound of seagulls and the rhythmic crash of waves against the harbour wall. St. Ives was stirring to life, and so was she. After a quick breakfast of tea and toast, she tied her hair back, grabbed her jacket, and stepped out of the café. Today, she resolved, would be the day she started getting to know her new surroundings and the people who called this town home.

Her first stop was the bookshop next door, which she had barely noticed during her errands the day before. The faded sign above the door read *The Book Nook*, and the small windows were cluttered with books of all shapes and sizes, along with a curious assortment of knickknacks: an old ship's compass, a framed map of Cornwall, and a model of a lighthouse.

The bell above the door jingled as Rosie stepped inside. The shop smelled of old paper and polished wood, a warm and inviting scent. Bookshelves towered over her, packed tightly with volumes ranging from classic literature to glossy travel guides. A cat, a large, fluffy tabby was curled up on the counter, its tail flicking lazily as it regarded her with half-closed eyes.

"Can I help you?"

The voice startled her, low and gravelly, coming from behind a shelf. A man emerged, his weathered face partially obscured by a scruffy beard. He wore a cardigan over a plaid shirt and jeans, and his expression was one of vague irritation, as though her presence had interrupted something important.

"I'm sorry to bother you," Rosie said quickly. "I'm your new neighbours. I've just inherited May's Haven."

The man's bushy eyebrows lifted slightly. "May's niece, are you?"

Rosie nodded. "Yes. Rosie Miller."

He studied her for a moment, then gave a curt nod. "Charlie mentioned you stopped by the hardware shop yesterday. I'm Owen."

"Nice to meet you, Owen," Rosie said, smiling.

Owen grunted, his gaze shifting to the cat. "That's Monty. He doesn't like strangers, but he'll tolerate you if you're quiet."

Rosie stifled a laugh. "Good to know. I'll try to stay on his good side."

Owen folded his arms, leaning against the counter. "So, what are you planning to do with May's place? Sell it off?"

"I'm not sure yet," Rosie admitted. "I thought I'd stay for a while and see if it feels right to keep it. Maybe even reopen the café."

At this, Owen's expression softened, though he still looked skeptical. "That place meant a lot to May. Be a shame to see it go."

"I feel the same way," Rosie said. "She must have loved it here."

Owen nodded. "She did. May was...well, she was May. Always full of ideas, always on the go. This town hasn't been the same without her."

Rosie felt a pang of sadness. She had only just begun to understand how deeply her aunt had been connected to this community. "I'd like to honour her memory," she said softly.

Owen's gaze lingered on her for a moment before he nodded again. "If you need anything, books, maps, or just someone to complain to, I'm here."

"Thank you," Rosie said, genuinely touched.

She left the shop feeling as though she had taken the first step toward becoming part of the town's fabric.

Rosie wandered through the narrow streets, taking in the sights and sounds of the bustling harbour town. St. Ives was alive with activity: fishermen unloading their catch, shopkeepers arranging their displays, and tourists snapping photos of the picturesque views.

She followed the smell of freshly baked bread to the town square, where a small market was set up. Stalls sold everything from local produce to handmade jewellery, and Rosie couldn't resist stopping to browse.

"Try this, love," said an elderly woman behind one of the stalls, holding out a slice of cheese on a toothpick. "Cornish Yarg. Best you'll find."

Rosie accepted the offering, savouring the creamy, tangy flavour. "It's delicious," she said.

"Glad you think so," the woman said with a grin. "You're new in town, aren't you?"

"Yes, I've just inherited May's Haven," Rosie replied.

The woman's eyes lit up. "Ah, May's niece! I'm Margaret. I used to help May with the café on busy weekends. She always said it was her little slice of heaven."

Rosie smiled. "That's what I've heard. I'm hoping to bring it back to life, though it's a bit daunting."

"You'll do fine, love," Margaret said, patting her hand. "And if you need help, just ask. We're all rooting for you."

Finding May's Journal

THAT AFTERNOON, ROSIE returned to the café and decided to tackle the task of sorting through the cluttered back room. It was filled with boxes of papers, old photographs, and other odds and ends that May had left behind.

As she sifted through the boxes, Rosie found herself smiling at the sheer variety of things her aunt had collected: postcards from all over the world, dried flowers pressed between the pages of books, and even a stack of menus from the café's earliest days.

But it was a worn leather-bound journal that caught her attention. Rosie opened it carefully, her breath catching as she recognised May's handwriting.

The journal was a mixture of recipes, sketches, and musings about the café. As Rosie flipped through the pages, she felt as though she were hearing her aunt's voice again.

• The café should feel like a warm hug, a place where people can come in from the cold and leave their worries at the door.

• Thinking of adding a reading corner with books for customers to borrow. Maybe Owen would donate a few from his shop.

• Tried a new scone recipe today, apple and cinnamon. Needs more spice, I think.

Rosie's heart swelled as she read. May had poured so much of herself into this place, dreaming of ways to make it not just a business but a haven for the community.

Near the end of the journal, Rosie found a passage that stopped her in her tracks:

• If anything ever happens to me, I hope Rosie finds her way here. She's got the heart for this kind of work, even if she doesn't know it yet.

Tears pricked at Rosie's eyes. May had believed in her, even from afar. It was a humbling and deeply moving realisation.

That evening, as Rosie sat by the window with a cup of tea, the journal open on the table before her, she felt a renewed sense of purpose.

May had seen something in her, something Rosie was only just beginning to see in herself.

Reopening the café wouldn't be easy, but it felt like the right thing to do. Not just for May, but for herself.

As the sun dipped below the horizon, painting the harbour in shades of gold and pink, Rosie made a silent promise.

"I'll give it my best, May," she whispered. "For you and for me."

The decision to stay and reopen May's Haven had been made, and Rosie was determined to see it through. But as she stood in the middle of the dusty café the next morning, surrounded by peeling paint and sagging shelves, she realised just how much work lay ahead.

Emily arrived shortly after, armed with cleaning supplies, paint samples, and her trademark enthusiasm. "Alright, Mum," she said, clapping her hands together. "Where do we start?"

Rosie looked around, feeling a little overwhelmed. "Everywhere," she said with a nervous laugh.

Clearing the Clutter

THE FIRST STEP WAS clearing out decades of accumulated clutter. Rosie and Emily tackled the back room, sorting through stacks of old menus, faded promotional posters, and boxes of miscellaneous odds and ends.

"Look at this!" Emily said, holding up a cracked teapot shaped like a lobster.

Rosie laughed. "That must have been one of May's treasures. She always had a soft spot for quirky things."

They created piles for items to keep, donate, and toss. By the end of the day, the back room was nearly empty, leaving only the essentials: shelves for storage, a sturdy work table, and a filing cabinet that Rosie planned to organise later.

"I didn't realised how much stuff was crammed in here," Rosie said, wiping her brow.

Emily grinned. "It's like a time capsule. But at least now we have space to work."

With the clutter cleared, the next step was deciding on a vision for the café. Rosie wanted to keep the cozy, welcoming atmosphere that May had created, but she also wanted to give it a fresh, modern feel.

Emily spread out a selection of paint swatches and fabric samples on one of the café tables. "I was thinking something light and cheerful," she said. "Like this pale yellow for the walls, and maybe these blue-and-white striped cushions for the chairs."

Rosie studied the samples, imagining how they would look in the space. "I like the yellow," she said. "It reminds me of sunshine."

"And it'll brighten the place up," Emily added. "What about the floors? They're looking a bit worse for wear."

Rosie glanced down at the scuffed wooden planks. "We'll have to sand them down and give them a new coat of varnish. It's a big job, but I think it'll be worth it."

They made a list of everything they needed: paint, brushes, varnish, new light fixtures, and fabric for the cushions. As Rosie reviewed the list, she couldn't help but feel a twinge of anxiety.

"This is going to be expensive," she said, frowning.

Emily placed a reassuring hand on her shoulder. "We'll take it one step at a time, Mum. And if we run into any trouble, we can always ask for help."

The next morning, as Rosie was sweeping the floor, the bell above the door jingled. She looked up to see Owen, the gruff bookshop owner, standing in the doorway with a toolbox in hand.

"Thought you might need this," he said, holding up a wrench.

Rosie smiled, grateful for the gesture. "Thank you, Owen. I was just thinking about tackling the leaky tap in the kitchen."

"I'll take care of it," Owen said gruffly. "No sense in you breaking something and making it worse."

Despite his brusque manner, Owen proved to be a skilled handyman. He fixed the tap, adjusted a creaky door hinge, and even helped Rosie replace a few loose floorboards.

"You've got your work cut out for you," he said as he packed up his tools.

"I know," Rosie said with a sigh. "But I'm determined to make this place shine again."

Owen gave her a rare smile. "May would be proud. She always said you had more grit than you gave yourself credit for."

The words warmed Rosie's heart, and she felt a renewed sense of determination.

AS THE RENOVATIONS progressed, Rosie began to encounter the inevitable hurdles.

One afternoon, as she and Emily were painting the walls, Rosie noticed a damp patch in the corner.

"What's that?" Emily asked, frowning.

Rosie sighed. "Looks like a leak. We'll need to get someone in to take a look."

The plumber's visit confirmed her fears: the pipework was old and needed replacing, which would cost more than she had budgeted for.

"It's one thing after another," Rosie said, sinking into a chair after the plumber left. "What if I've bitten off more than I can chew?"

Emily knelt beside her, her expression serious but supportive. "Mum, every project has its challenges. You're doing an amazing job, and we'll figure this out. Maybe we can cut costs somewhere else or spread the work out over a longer period."

Rosie nodded, though she still felt the weight of the financial strain.

Doubts and Encouragement

THAT EVENING, AS ROSIE sat alone in the upstairs flat, she found herself questioning whether she had made the right decision. The café felt like a mountain she wasn't sure she could climb, and the financial setbacks only added to her doubts.

She pulled out May's journal, hoping to find some reassurance.

• There will always be obstacles, but don't let them stop you. The best things in life are worth fighting for.

Rosie smiled through her tears. May's words were exactly what she needed to hear.

The next day, Rosie was surprised to find Margaret, the cheese vendor from the market, standing outside the café with a basket of sandwiches and pastries.

"Thought you might need a bit of fuel," Margaret said with a grin.

"Thank you," Rosie said, touched by the gesture.

As word spread about Rosie's plans, more locals began to offer their support. Charlie from the hardware store donated some leftover paint, and Owen continued to lend his handyman skills whenever he could.

Even Monty, the bookshop cat, became a regular visitor, lounging on the café counter as Rosie and Emily worked.

"It feels like the whole town wants you to succeed," Emily said one afternoon as they sanded the floors.

Rosie smiled, feeling a sense of connection to the community that she hadn't felt in years.

By the end of the third week, the café was beginning to take shape. The walls were freshly painted, the floors gleamed with a new coat of varnish, and the furniture had been scrubbed and polished. Rosie and Emily had even sewn new cushions for the chairs, using the blue-and-white striped fabric they had chosen.

As they stepped back to admire their work, Rosie felt a surge of pride.

"It's starting to look like a real café again," she said.

Emily grinned. "It's more than a café, Mum. It's a dream come to life."

Rosie nodded, her heart swelling with hope. There was still work to be done, but for the first time, she could see the finish line.

And she knew that May's Haven was exactly where she was meant to be.

The hum of the oven filled the café kitchen, accompanied by the rhythmic sound of Rosie's knife slicing through fresh apples. The morning sun streamed through the windows, bathing the room in a warm glow as Rosie worked. A light dusting of flour covered the counter, and the sweet aroma of cinnamon and butter filled the air.

It had been years since she had baked anything more complicated than a tray of biscuits, but now, as Rosie stood in the middle of May's Haven's kitchen, her love for cooking was slowly returning. At first, it had felt daunting to step back into the kitchen and try her hand at the recipes her aunt had perfected over the years. But as she thumbed through May's journal, filled with scribbled notes and annotated recipes, she found herself inspired.

"Alright," Rosie murmured to herself, glancing at the recipe for *Spiced Apple Scones*. "Let's see if I've still got it."

Rediscovering a Passion

BAKING BECAME ROSIE'S way of grounding herself amid the chaos of renovations. Each morning, she would choose a recipe from May's journal, gather the ingredients, and spend a few hours experimenting. Some days, the results were marvellous, fluffy scones, delicate lemon tarts, perfectly crisp biscuits. Other days, the outcomes were less successful, but Rosie took the failures in stride.

She found joy in the process, the smell of freshly baked bread, the satisfying crackle of a golden crust, the simple pleasure of kneading dough with her hands. It reminded her of the early days of her marriage, when she and Tom would spend weekends baking together, filling the house with laughter and the smell of vanilla.

As the days passed, Rosie grew bolder in her experiments. She tweaked recipes, adding her own twists to May's classics. A simple Victoria sponge became a zesty orange-and-cardamom cake. Her apple scones transformed into blackberry and thyme.

Emily became her enthusiastic taste tester, stopping by after work to sample the day's creations.

"This is amazing, Mum," Emily said one evening, biting into a gooey chocolate tart. "You've got a real gift, you know."

Rosie smiled, her cheeks flushing with pride. "It's May's recipes. She knew what she was doing."

"It's more than that," Emily insisted. "You've made them your own. People are going to love this when the café opens."

One crisp autumn morning, Rosie was sweeping the front steps of the café when she noticed a man standing across the street, studying the building with a curious expression. He was tall and broad-shouldered, with salt-and-pepper hair and a tool belt slung low around his waist.

"Can I help you?" Rosie called, setting the broom aside.

The man crossed the street, his boots crunching on the cobblestones. "Sorry to bother you," he said, his voice warm and rich. "I'm Sam. Sam Harper. I heard you're fixing up May's Haven."

"That's right," Rosie said, extending her hand. "I'm Rosie Miller, May's niece."

Sam shook her hand, his grip firm but gentle. "I knew May," he said. "I'm a retired carpenter now, but back when I was still working, I helped her with a few projects around the café. She always said this place was her pride and joy."

Rosie smiled. "It was. I'm hoping to bring it back to life, though it's been a bit of a challenge."

Sam's eyes crinkled at the corners as he smiled. "I can imagine. These old buildings have a way of surprising you."

"Tell me about it," Rosie said with a laugh. "Just last week, I discovered the plumbing needs a complete overhaul."

"Well, if you need an extra pair of hands, I'd be happy to help," Sam offered. "I've got some time on my hands these days, and it would be nice to see the café back in business."

Rosie hesitated for a moment, but there was something reassuring about Sam's easy manner. "That would be wonderful," she said. "Thank you."

Sam proved to be an invaluable addition to the renovations. With his expertise, they tackled some of the more challenging tasks, from repairing the warped wooden counter to building new shelves for the back room.

One afternoon, as they worked side by side sanding down a table, Rosie found herself laughing at one of Sam's stories about his early days as a carpenter.

"And then," Sam said, chuckling, "the whole cabinet collapsed, right in front of the client. I've never been so embarrassed in my life."

Rosie laughed, wiping sawdust from her hands. "Sounds like you survived, though."

"Barely," Sam said with a grin. "But you learn more from your mistakes than your successes, don't you?"

Rosie nodded, her smile fading slightly. "I suppose you do."

Sam glanced at her, his expression softening. "You're doing something incredible here, Rosie. I hope you know that."

She looked down at the table, her cheeks flushing. "I'm just trying to make something of May's legacy. It's not easy, though. Sometimes I wonder if I'm in over my head."

Sam reached over and gently squeezed her shoulder. "You're not. This place already has so much heart, and that's because of you. Keep going, you're doing just fine."

As the renovations progressed, Rosie found herself growing closer to the people of St. Ives. Margaret continued to drop by with sandwiches and encouragement, and Owen from the bookshop became a regular fixture, often bringing Monty with him.

Sam, however, became her most constant companion. He had a knack for making even the most tedious tasks enjoyable, and his quiet confidence helped steady Rosie's own doubts.

One evening, after a long day of painting, Sam and Rosie sat on the steps of the café, sharing a thermos of tea. The harbour was bathed in golden light, and the sound of the waves was soothing.

"You ever think about what May would say if she saw this?" Sam asked, gesturing toward the café.

Rosie smiled. "I think she'd be proud. But she'd also have a hundred suggestions for how to do it better."

Sam chuckled. "Sounds about right."

They sat in comfortable silence for a moment before Sam spoke again. "You're doing more than just fixing up a building, you know. You're building something for yourself. Something that matters."

Rosie's chest tightened, but it wasn't the painful ache of doubt she had felt in the past. It was something warmer, something hopeful.

"Thank you, Sam," she said softly.

He smiled at her, and for a moment, the world seemed to still.

<u>Testing Recipes with Friends</u>

AS THE RENOVATIONS neared completion, Rosie decided it was time to start testing her recipes on an audience. She invited Emily, Sam, Margaret, and Owen to the café one evening, setting up a small buffet of cakes, scones, and sandwiches.

"This is a trial run," Rosie said nervously as her friends filled their plates. "Be honest, if something's terrible, I want to know."

Margaret took a bite of a lemon drizzle cake and sighed contentedly. "If this is terrible, I don't want to know what good is," she said.

Owen nodded in agreement, his mouth full of blackberry scone. "You've outdone yourself, Rosie."

Sam raised his cup of tea in a toast. "To Rosie and to May's Haven."

The group cheered, and Rosie felt a swell of pride and gratitude. For the first time, she truly believed that she could make this dream a reality.

As the evening wound down and the others began to leave, Sam lingered behind to help Rosie tidy up.

"Thanks for tonight," Rosie said as they stacked plates in the kitchen. "It really means a lot to me."

"You don't need to thank me," Sam said, leaning against the counter. "I'm just glad I get to be part of this."

Their eyes met, and for a moment, the air between them felt charged with something unspoken. Rosie looked away, her heart fluttering.

"Well," she said, clearing her throat. "I'd better finish up here."

Sam nodded, but as he left, he paused in the doorway. "Goodnight, Rosie."

"Goodnight, Sam," she replied, her voice soft.

As the door closed behind him, Rosie couldn't help but smile.

Rosie was growing more confident every day, not just in her baking and her ability to run the café, but in herself. May's Haven was becoming more than just a project. It was becoming home.

The Grand Opening of Rosie's Café

THE MORNING OF THE grand opening dawned crisp and clear, with a salty breeze rolling in from the harbour. Rosie stood outside *May's Haven*, her hands wrapped tightly around a mug of tea. The café's new sign, freshly painted and gleaming, swayed gently in the breeze. *Rosie's Café*, it now read, in bold, cheerful script. Beneath it, in smaller letters, was the dedication: *In Loving Memory of May Evans.*

Rosie took a deep breath, trying to calm the butterflies in her stomach. The past weeks had been a whirlwind of preparation, testing recipes, polishing the floors until they gleamed, arranging flowers on every table, but now, as the moment arrived, doubt crept in. What if no one came? Or worse, what if they came and didn't like it?

Her thoughts were interrupted by Emily, who emerged from the café carrying a tray of freshly baked scones. "Stop fretting, Mum," she said with a grin. "It's going to be perfect."

Rosie smiled, though her nerves still buzzed. "I just want everything to go smoothly."

"And it will," Emily said firmly. "Now, come on. Let's get everything ready."

The café's doors opened at 9 a.m., and Rosie was both thrilled and overwhelmed to see a small line of customers already waiting outside. Margaret was first in line, followed closely by Owen and Monty, who sauntered in like he owned the place.

"Morning, Rosie!" Margaret called. "Hope you're ready for us!"

Rosie laughed, her nerves easing slightly. "Come on in!"

Within an hour, the café was bustling. Locals and tourists filled the tables, chatting over steaming cups of tea and plates of Rosie's homemade scones. The air was filled with the comforting hum of conversation, punctuated by the clink of cups and the occasional bark of laughter.

But behind the counter, chaos reigned. Rosie and Emily rushed to keep up with orders, dodging each other as they moved between the kitchen and the front counter.

"We need three more coffees for table six!" Emily called, balancing a tray of pastries.

"Got it!" Rosie replied, frantically pouring milk into a cappuccino.

Sam appeared in the doorway, a broad grin on his face. "Need a hand?"

"Desperately," Rosie said, laughing despite herself.

Sam rolled up his sleeves and jumped in, clearing tables and delivering orders with the ease of someone who had worked in hospitality his entire life. His presence steadied Rosie, and gradually, the chaos began to feel more manageable.

Of course, not everything went perfectly. The coffee machine sputtered and nearly broke halfway through the morning rush, and Rosie burned a batch of scones while trying to juggle too many tasks at once.

At one point, a child spilled a glass of orange juice all over the freshly varnished floor, and Rosie nearly slipped while trying to clean it up.

But through it all, the customers remained patient and kind. Margaret stepped behind the counter to help pour tea, and Owen took charge of calming the child who had spilled the juice.

"Don't worry, Rosie," Margaret said with a wink. "No grand opening goes off without a hitch. You're doing brilliantly."

A Moment of Reflection

BY MID-AFTERNOON, THE rush had slowed, and Rosie finally had a moment to catch her breath. She stood behind the counter, surveying the café. Sunlight streamed through the freshly cleaned windows, illuminating the happy faces of her customers. The air was filled with the scent of cinnamon and coffee, and the soft murmur of conversation created a warm, inviting atmosphere.

Emily appeared beside her, handing her a cup of tea. "You did it, Mum," she said, her voice filled with pride.

Rosie smiled, her chest swelling with emotion. "We did it," she corrected, squeezing Emily's hand.

Sam approached, wiping his hands on a towel. "Looks like it's a hit," he said, nodding toward the bustling tables.

Rosie nodded, her eyes misting slightly. "I can't believe how many people showed up. It's...it's more than I ever hoped for."

"You deserve it," Sam said softly.

As the day wound down, Rosie stood in front of the café and addressed the remaining customers.

"Thank you all for coming today," she began, her voice trembling slightly. "This café isn't just a business to me—it's a legacy. My Aunt May poured her heart and soul into this place, and I'm honoured to carry it forward. None of this would have been possible without the support of my family, my friends, and this incredible community. Thank you, from the bottom of my heart."

The crowd erupted into applause, and Rosie felt tears prick her eyes.

That evening, after the café had been cleaned and locked up, Rosie sat on the steps outside, gazing out at the harbour. The water shimmered under the light of the moon, and the air was cool and crisp.

Emily and Sam joined her, each carrying a cup of tea.

"You did something amazing today, Mum," Emily said, leaning her head on Rosie's shoulder.

"I still can't believe it," Rosie admitted. "I was so scared no one would come."

"But they did," Sam said, his voice steady. "And they'll keep coming. You've created something special here, Rosie."

Rosie smiled, her heart full. For the first time in years, she felt truly at peace. She had taken a leap of faith, and it had paid off.

May's Haven had become Rosie's Café, and with it, Rosie had found a renewed sense of purpose and a place where she truly belonged.

Personal Growth and Reflection

THE WEEKS FOLLOWING the grand opening of Rosie's Café passed in a blur of busy mornings, long afternoons, and quiet, contemplative evenings. The café had quickly become a fixture in St. Ives, attracting both locals and tourists alike with its warm atmosphere and Rosie's signature baked goods. Yet, amid the steady hum of her new life, Rosie found herself pausing more and more to reflect on how far she had come.

She often woke early, before the sun had fully risen, and sat by the window of her upstairs flat, a steaming cup of tea in hand. It was during these still moments that her thoughts drifted back to the past, to the life she had left behind, the love she had lost, and the woman she was slowly rediscovering.

One chilly morning, Rosie sat wrapped in a blanket, watching the waves crash against the harbour wall. The sky was streaked with pale pinks and oranges, and the world felt hushed, as if holding its breath.

Her mind wandered back to Tom. Two years had passed since his death, yet his absence still felt raw at times, like a wound that had only begun to heal. She thought of the mornings they used to spend together, sipping coffee in their garden, sharing quiet conversations about everything and nothing.

"Tom," she murmured softly, her voice barely audible over the sound of the sea. "I wish you could see me now."

She imagined what he might say if he were here, how his eyes would crinkle at the corners as he teased her about running a café. But she also knew he would be proud, proud of the risks she had taken, the courage she had found, and the life she was building for herself.

It wasn't that she had moved on from Tom, she doubted she ever truly would, but she was learning to carry her love for him in a new way. It was no longer a weight that held her back but a steady presence that guided her forward.

A Visit from Peter

ONE SATURDAY AFTERNOON, as the café was winding down for the day, Rosie looked up to see a familiar face standing in the doorway.

"Peter!" she exclaimed, her heart leaping with surprise and joy.

Her son, tall and sharp-featured, stepped inside with a sheepish smile. "Hi, Mum. Thought I'd come and see the famous Rosie's Café for myself."

Rosie hurried around the counter to hug him, her arms wrapping tightly around his broad shoulders. "I didn't know you were coming!"

"I wanted to surprise you," Peter said, glancing around the café. "This place is amazing, Mum. You've really done something special here."

Rosie beamed, her chest swelling with pride. "It's been a lot of work, but it's worth it."

Peter ordered a coffee and sat at one of the corner tables, watching as Rosie bustled about. She noticed the way his gaze softened when he saw her interacting with customers, how he seemed genuinely impressed by the café's charm and success.

As the last few customers left and the café quieted, Peter helped her stack chairs and wipe down tables.

"You know," he said as they worked, "I wasn't sure about this at first. When Emily told me about the café, I worried it would be too much for you. But seeing you here...it's like you're in your element."

Rosie paused, her cloth still in hand, and looked at her son. "I was scared too," she admitted. "For a long time, I didn't think I could do this. But being here, it's changed something in me. I feel like I'm finally living again, Peter. Really living."

Peter nodded, his expression thoughtful. "I'm proud of you, Mum. Dad would be too."

Rosie's eyes filled with tears, but they were tears of gratitude. "Thank you, love. That means more to me than you know."

The following weekend, Emily joined Peter and Rosie for a family dinner in the flat above the café. Rosie had cooked one of her aunt May's favourite dishes, a rich fish pie topped with buttery mashed potatoes and the three of them sat around the small kitchen table, laughing and sharing stories.

"It's strange," Peter said as he helped himself to a second serving. "I feel like I'm seeing a whole new side of you, Mum."

Rosie smiled, her heart warm. "Maybe it's a side of me that's always been there, but I just didn't have the chance to show it."

Emily raised her glass of wine. "To Mum and to new beginnings."

Peter joined the toast, and Rosie felt a lump rise in her throat as their glasses clinked. She couldn't remember the last time she had felt so content, so connected to her children and to herself.

After dinner, Peter headed back to his hotel, leaving Rosie and Emily to tidy up the kitchen. As they washed the dishes, Emily turned to her mother with a soft smile.

"You've changed, Mum," she said.

Rosie raised an eyebrow. "Changed? How so?"

"You're...lighter," Emily said, searching for the right word. "Happier. More confident. It's like you've found a part of yourself that was missing."

Rosie paused, drying a plate with a towel. "I think I have," she said. "For so long, I felt lost without your dad. I didn't know who I was or what I wanted. But coming here, starting the café, it's helped me remember who I am. And it's given me something to look forward to again."

Emily's eyes filled with tears, and she reached over to squeeze her mother's hand. "I'm so proud of you, Mum. I hope you know that."

Rosie smiled, her own eyes misting. "I do. And I'm so grateful for you and Peter. I couldn't have done this without you."

That night, as Rosie lay in bed, she thought about the journey that had brought her here, the grief, the doubts, the moments of joy and triumph. She thought about May, whose legacy had sparked this new life.

Settling Into the Café Life

THE MONTHS AFTER THE café's grand opening were a whirlwind of activity for Rosie. Every day brought new challenges, new faces, and new opportunities to grow into her role as the owner of Rosie's Café. What had once seemed like an overwhelming responsibility had now become her greatest joy.

The daily bustle of the café filled her with purpose. From the moment she unlocked the doors in the morning to the quiet hours of cleaning up in the evening, Rosie found herself falling into the rhythm of her new life. But beyond the work itself, what truly energised her was the way the café was becoming a hub for the community, just as her Aunt May had envisioned.

One of the first signs that Rosie's Café was making an impact came on a crisp autumn morning. Rosie was busy arranging a tray of scones when Margaret bustled in, carrying a basket of apples.

"These are from my garden," Margaret said, setting the basket on the counter. "Thought you might like to use them in one of your recipes."

Rosie's heart swelled with gratitude. "Thank you, Margaret. These will make a lovely apple tart."

Margaret smiled. "You've done more for this town in a few months than most people do in years. We're lucky to have you, Rosie."

Rosie flushed at the compliment. "I'm the lucky one," she said. "This place has given me so much more than I could have imagined."

As the weeks went on, more townspeople began to contribute to the café's success. Local artists donated paintings and photographs to brighten the walls, while the nearby florist provided fresh flowers for the tables. Rosie's Café was becoming more than just a business, it was a shared space where the community could come together.

One evening, Owen from the bookshop approached Rosie with an idea.

"I've been thinking," he said, sipping his tea. "What if we hosted a poetry reading here? There are a few local writers who'd love the chance to share their work, and your café would be the perfect setting."

Rosie hesitated. "A poetry reading? I'm not sure if people would be interested."

"They will," Owen said confidently. "You'd be surprised how many creative types live in this town."

Encouraged by his enthusiasm, Rosie agreed, and a week later, the café was transformed into a cozy venue for the event. Candles flickered on the tables, and the air was filled with the scent of spiced apple cider.

The turnout was better than Rosie had anticipated. Locals of all ages filled the café, listening intently as poets recited their work. Some of the poems were funny, others deeply moving, but all of them brought the room to life in a way Rosie hadn't expected.

As the evening came to an end, Owen approached her with a rare smile. "See? I told you it would be a hit."

Rosie laughed. "You were right. Let's do it again next month."

The success of the poetry reading inspired Rosie to host more events. She organised a baking class for children, a book club meeting in partnership with Owen's shop, and even a small Christmas market in the café's courtyard. Each event brought more people through the doors, strengthening the sense of community that was growing around Rosie's Café.

As the café grew busier, Rosie realised she needed extra help. Emily suggested putting up a sign in the window to advertise for a part-time barista, and within a few days, Rosie had received several applications.

One applicant stood out: a quiet but eager young woman named Chloe, who had recently finished school and was unsure of what to do next.

"I've never worked in a café before," Chloe admitted during the interview, her hands twisting nervously in her lap. "But I'm a fast learner, and I love coffee."

Rosie saw something of herself in Chloe, a mix of uncertainty and determination and decided to give her a chance.

On Chloe's first day, Rosie showed her how to use the coffee machine, explaining the difference between a cappuccino and a latte.

"It's all about practice," Rosie said as Chloe nervously frothed milk for the first time. "Don't worry if it's not perfect right away. You'll get the hang of it."

Over time, Chloe became more confident in her role, and Rosie found herself taking on the role of a mentor. She taught Chloe how to bake the café's signature scones, how to greet customers with warmth, and how to handle the occasional grumpy patron with grace.

"You've got a real knack for this," Rosie said one afternoon as they worked side by side in the kitchen.

Chloe blushed. "Thanks, Rosie. I've learned so much from you. I never thought I'd enjoy this kind of work, but now I can't imagine doing anything else."

Rosie felt a surge of pride. Helping Chloe discover her potential was one of the most rewarding parts of her new life.

As the months passed, Rosie settled into the daily rhythm of café life. She loved the way the mornings started quietly, with the smell of freshly brewed coffee filling the air, before gradually building into a lively buzz of conversation and laughter.

She knew the regulars by name and had memorised their favourite orders. Margaret always came in for a pot of Earl Grey and a slice of lemon drizzle cake, while Charlie from the hardware store preferred a strong black coffee and a bacon sandwich.

Even the tourists, who came and went with the seasons, brought their own charm to the café. Rosie loved hearing their stories, where they had traveled from, what had drawn them to St. Ives and she took pride in making them feel at home.

One evening, as Rosie sat in the empty café after closing, she reflected on how much her life had changed.

When she first arrived in St. Ives, she had been filled with doubt, doubt about her abilities, doubt about her place in the world, doubt about whether she could ever truly move forward after Tom's death.

Now, she felt like a different person. She was no longer defined by her grief or her fears. She was part of something bigger, a community that valued her, a café that brought people together, and a life that felt full of possibility.

As she turned off the lights and locked the door, Rosie felt a sense of contentment that had eluded her for so long. She was exactly where she was meant to be.

The cozy warmth of Rosie's Café had become a cornerstone of St. Ives. Regulars came for the comfort of her freshly baked scones, the cheerful yellow walls, and the sense of community that filled the space. But one chilly Tuesday morning, Rosie stood at the counter, reading a folded leaflet that Owen had just dropped off with a grim expression.

"Thought you'd want to see this," he said, nodding toward the paper in her hands.

The leaflet was glossy and colourful, announcing the grand opening of a new café just a few streets away. *Seaside Brews* boasted artisanal coffee, trendy vegan snacks, and a sleek, modern interior. The opening date was set for next week, and the flyer offered free drinks for the first 100 customers.

Rosie's heart sank. Competition wasn't entirely unexpected, St. Ives was a tourist town, after all, but the slick presentation of Seaside

Brews felt like a direct challenge to the quaint, homey atmosphere she had worked so hard to cultivate.

"What do you think?" Owen asked, leaning against the counter.

Rosie sighed. "I think this could be trouble."

<u>*The Threat of Competition*</u>

Over the next week, the buzz surrounding Seaside Brews grew louder. Flyers appeared in shop windows across town, and social media posts from excited locals filled Rosie's news feed. The new café promised a chic alternative to the traditional tearooms that dominated St. Ives, and many were eager to see what it had to offer.

Rosie tried to focus on her own work, but the looming competition weighed heavily on her mind.

One morning, as she served a regular customer their usual pot of Earl Grey, Margaret leaned in conspiratorially. "Have you heard about that new place?"

"I have," Rosie admitted.

Margaret sniffed. "All style and no substance, if you ask me. Don't let it bother you, love. People know quality when they see it."

Rosie forced a smile, but doubts gnawed at her. What if Margaret was wrong? What if people preferred Seaside Brews' trendy aesthetic to her cozy, traditional café?

When Seaside Brews opened, Rosie's fears became a reality. Foot traffic in her café slowed noticeably, especially during the mid-morning rush when tourists and locals alike were drawn to the allure of free coffee and Instagram-worthy interiors.

Chloe, her young barista, frowned as she wiped down an already clean counter. "It's quiet today," she said, glancing at the nearly empty café.

Rosie nodded, her chest tight. "It's the new place. People are curious."

Chloe hesitated before speaking. "They'll come back, Rosie. This café has something special, you."

Rosie smiled weakly. She appreciated Chloe's optimism, but the quieter days only deepened her doubts.

One evening, after closing the café, Rosie sat in the kitchen with Emily, venting her frustrations over a glass of wine.

"I feel like I'm losing everything I've worked so hard for," Rosie admitted, her voice shaking. "What if I can't compete with them? What if this café isn't enough?"

Emily reached across the table, squeezing her mother's hand. "Mum, you've built something incredible here. People don't come to Rosie's Café just for the coffee or the cakes, they come because of you. They come because this place feels like home."

"But is that enough?" Rosie asked quietly.

Emily's eyes softened. "It will be if you believe in it. You've faced challenges before, and you've always found a way through. This is no different."

That night, Rosie lay awake, staring at the ceiling. Emily's words echoed in her mind, but so did the creeping doubt that had plagued her since Seaside Brews opened.

She thought about Aunt May's journal, the handwritten recipes, and the dreams May had poured into the café. Slowly, an idea began to take shape.

The next morning, Rosie arrived at the café early, determined to take action. She pulled out May's journal and flipped through its pages until she found what she was looking for: a section labeled *Community Events*.

The café is more than a place to eat or drink, it's a gathering space, a hub for the town. Host events. Make people feel like they're part of something special.

Rosie smiled to herself. She had been so focused on surviving the competition that she had forgotten what made her café unique: its sense of community.

Over the next week, Rosie began implementing her plan. She started by introducing a series of themed events at the café.

- **Baking Nights**: Customers could learn to bake her signature scones and pies in small, intimate workshops.
- **Live Music Fridays**: Local musicians were invited to perform, turning the café into a lively, welcoming space in the evenings.
- **Family Story time**: Parents and children gathered on Saturday mornings for stories and activities, with tea and biscuits included.

Rosie also revamped her menu, adding new seasonal items inspired by May's recipes. She sourced fresh ingredients from local farmers and added personal touches to every dish, from hand-lettered menus to little jars of homemade jam on each table.

"People need a reason to choose us," Rosie explained to Chloe as they worked together one evening. "We're not just selling coffee, we're offering an experience, something they can't get anywhere else."

At first, the changes were slow to take effect. Rosie worried that her efforts wouldn't be enough to bring people back. But gradually, word began to spread.

The baking workshops filled up quickly, with participants raving about the experience on social media. Families flocked to the café for story time, and the live music nights drew a diverse crowd of locals and tourists.

Margaret stopped by one morning to share her thoughts. "This place feels alive again," she said, sipping her tea. "You've reminded people why they loved it here in the first place."

Rosie smiled, feeling a flicker of hope.

On quiet evenings, when the café was closed and Rosie sat alone with her thoughts, Tiggy was always there. She would leap onto Rosie's lap, her purrs filling the silence, and remind her that no matter how busy or challenging the day had been, she was never truly alone.

Tiggy had a way of grounding Rosie, of reminding her to pause and appreciate the small moments: the warmth of a cup of tea, the glow of the sunset, or the simple joy of having someone—or some *cat*—who loved her unconditionally.

For Rosie, Tiggy wasn't just a pet. She was family, a reminder of resilience and companionship as she embraced her new life in St. Ives.

Facing the Competition Head-On

ONE AFTERNOON, ROSIE decided to visit Seaside Brews. She wanted to see what she was up against, to understand why people were so drawn to the new café.

The space was sleek and modern, with minimalist décor and a polished menu. The coffee was excellent, and the staff were friendly, but as Rosie sat at a table, she couldn't help but feel that something was missing.

The café was beautiful, but it lacked warmth. It felt like a place to pass through, not a place to stay.

Rosie returned to her own café that evening with a renewed sense of purpose. She didn't need to compete with Seaside Brews by trying to mimic their style, she just needed to double down on what made Rosie's Café special: its heart.

In the weeks that followed, Rosie began to trust her instincts more. She stopped worrying about what the competition was doing and focused on her own vision for the café.

One evening, after a particularly successful baking workshop, Sam joined her in the kitchen for a cup of tea.

"You've done something incredible here," he said, his voice full of admiration.

Rosie smiled. "I've had my doubts, but I think I'm finally starting to believe in myself."

"You should," Sam said. "You've turned this place into more than just a café, you've turned it into a home."

Rosie felt a warmth spread through her chest. She still had challenges to face, but she knew she was capable of overcoming them.

With the support of her community, her family, and her own resilience, Rosie was ready for whatever came next.

The sun was beginning to set over the harbour as Rosie locked the front door of her café, her hands lingering on the cool brass handle. The day had been long but satisfying, another baking workshop, a bustling lunch service, and the steady hum of laughter and conversation from her customers. Yet, as the harbour lights flickered on and the sea breeze cooled the air, she realised the café wasn't the only thing on her mind.

It was Sam.

The retired carpenter had become a constant presence in her life over the past few months, always ready to help with a broken chair leg or to lend a hand during the café's busy hours. But it wasn't just his practicality that Rosie appreciated. It was the quiet steadiness he brought, the easy way they slipped into conversation, and the warmth in his smile that stayed with her long after he'd left.

Still, as much as she looked forward to his visits, the growing feelings she harboured for Sam filled her with both excitement and trepidation.

A Chance Invitation

THAT EVENING, AS ROSIE settled into her upstairs flat with a cup of tea, Tiggy on her lap, her phone buzzed on the counter. It was a message from Sam:

"Are you free tomorrow evening? I thought I'd take a crack at making fish pie. It won't be as good as yours, but I could use a taste-tester."

Rosie felt her heart skip a beat. She smiled, typing a quick reply:

"Sounds perfect. What time?"

The next evening, she found herself standing outside Sam's cottage, a bottle of wine in hand and a flutter of nerves in her chest. The door opened before she could knock, and Sam greeted her with a grin.

"Right on time," he said, stepping aside to let her in.

The cottage was cozy and inviting, with soft lighting and the faint smell of baking fish. Rosie took in the cluttered bookshelves, the worn but comfortable furniture, and the photographs of boats and beaches lining the walls. It felt lived-in and warm, much like Sam himself.

Over dinner, they talked easily, sharing stories of their lives before St. Ives. Rosie told Sam about her years with Tom, the joys and challenges of raising Emily and Peter, and the quiet life she had led before inheriting the café.

Sam, in turn, spoke of his years as a carpenter, his retirement, and the winding path that had brought him to St. Ives.

"You've created something special with that café," Sam said, his gaze steady. "It's not just a business, it's a part of this town now. And that's because of you."

Rosie felt a warmth spread through her chest. "I couldn't have done it without you," she said softly.

Sam shook his head. "You would've found your way, Rosie. You're stronger than you give yourself credit for."

For a moment, their eyes met, and the air between them seemed to shift. Rosie quickly looked away, her cheeks flushing.

As the weeks went on, Rosie and Sam's friendship deepened. They often spent evenings together, walking along the harbour, sharing meals, or simply talking about their days. Yet, beneath the surface of their growing closeness, Rosie felt a storm of emotions she wasn't sure how to navigate.

She hadn't allowed herself to imagine being with someone new after Tom's death. Their marriage had been one of quiet strength and deep love, and the idea of moving on had once seemed impossible. But Sam was different. He didn't try to replace Tom or fill the empty space he had left. Instead, he brought something new into Rosie's life, something that felt hopeful and exciting, but also terrifying.

One evening, as they walked along the beach, Sam stopped and turned to her.

"Rosie," he said, his voice gentle. "I know this is complicated, and I don't want to push you. But I care about you, more than just as a friend."

Rosie's heart raced, but she forced herself to meet his gaze. "I care about you too," she admitted. "But I...I'm scared, Sam. I've already lost someone I loved deeply, and the thought of opening myself up again—" She broke off, her voice trembling.

Sam reached for her hand, his touch steady and reassuring. "I can't promise life won't throw us curveballs," he said. "But I can promise to take it one step at a time, with you."

Rosie felt tears prick her eyes. It was the kind of patience and understanding she hadn't realised she needed.

"Okay," she said quietly. "One step at a time."

Sharing with Emily and Peter

THE FIRST REAL TEST of their budding relationship came when Emily and Peter visited the café for a family dinner. Rosie had decided it was time to tell her children about Sam, though the thought filled her with nerves.

After dessert, as they lingered over cups of tea, Rosie cleared her throat.

"There's something I want to tell you," she began, her voice careful. "I've been spending time with someone. His name is Sam, and he's become very important to me."

Emily's eyes lit up with curiosity. "Sam? The carpenter who helped with the café?"

Rosie nodded. "Yes. It's still new, but...it feels right."

Peter, always the more reserved of the two, set down his mug. "Mum, are you happy?"

Rosie smiled, her chest tightening with emotion. "I am. I didn't think I could feel this way again, but Sam has been so kind and patient. He makes me happy."

Emily reached across the table to squeeze her mother's hand. "Then we're happy for you, Mum. Dad would want you to find joy again."

Peter nodded, a small smile softening his features. "It's not easy to move forward, but you deserve this, Mum. We're proud of you."

Rosie felt tears slip down her cheeks, but they were tears of gratitude and love.

As the months went on, Rosie and Sam's relationship blossomed. They found joy in the simple things, sharing a meal, tackling a project at the café, or walking hand in hand along the beach.

There were moments of doubt and hesitation, but Sam's steady presence helped Rosie navigate the complexities of loving again. He didn't try to erase her past or compare himself to Tom. Instead, he honoured her journey and celebrated the life they were building together.

One evening, as they watched the sun set over the harbour, Rosie turned to Sam and said, "Thank you for being patient with me. I didn't think I'd find love again, but you've shown me that it's possible."

Sam smiled, wrapping his arm around her shoulders. "You've shown me the same thing, Rosie. And I wouldn't trade this for anything."

Rosie's journey with Sam wasn't about replacing the love she had lost. It was about embracing the possibility of joy, even after heartbreak.

With Sam by her side, Rosie felt more grounded and hopeful than ever. Together, they faced the challenges of running the café, supported their community, and built a life filled with love, laughter, and the promise of new beginnings.

As Rosie stood in the café one busy afternoon, watching Sam chat with a regular customer, she realised something: she had found not just a partner, but a kindred spirit, someone who made her feel like she was exactly where she was meant to be.

And for Rosie, that was enough.

A Fulfilling Resolution

THE SUN ROSE OVER ST. Ives, casting golden light over the harbour and painting the water in shimmering hues of blue and silver. The sound of gulls filled the air as Rosie stood outside *Rosie's Café*, her hands wrapped around a steaming mug of tea. She gazed out at the familiar view, her heart full as the town stirred to life.

The café had become more than she had ever imagined. It was no longer just a business but a vibrant hub for the community. The tables were rarely empty, and the air was often filled with the sounds of laughter, conversations, and the comforting clink of teacups. Rosie had poured her heart and soul into the place, and now, standing here, she knew it had all been worth it.

Inside the café, Chloe was already busy preparing for the morning rush. Over the months, she had blossomed into a confident and capable barista, and Rosie couldn't have been prouder.

"Morning, Rosie!" Chloe called, grinning as she poured a latte. "We've got a big reservation for the book club this afternoon."

Rosie chuckled. "Good thing we've stocked up on scones, then."

The book club had become one of the café's most popular events, drawing locals of all ages to discuss everything from classic novels to contemporary thrillers. Rosie had even convinced Owen to lead a few sessions, and his dry wit never failed to entertain the group.

The café was also home to the town's art nights, where local painters and sculptors displayed their work, and to Rosie's beloved baking workshops, which continued to draw aspiring bakers from across the region.

On Fridays, the café transformed into a cozy music venue, with live performances by local musicians. These evenings were Rosie's favourite. She loved seeing the tables filled with friends and neighbours, the room aglow with soft lighting, and the walls humming with the joy of shared experiences.

One morning, as Rosie bustled about the café, Margaret walked in with a wide grin on her face.

"Guess what, love?" she said, pulling out a newspaper and placing it on the counter.

Rosie's eyes widened as she saw the headline: "Rosie's Café: A Seaside Gem Bringing Life to St. Ives."

Underneath was a glowing review, praising the café's welcoming atmosphere, delicious food, and role in fostering community spirit.

"They've got it exactly right," Margaret said, beaming. "This place is the heart of the town now."

Rosie felt a lump rise in her throat. "Thank you, Margaret. I couldn't have done any of this without all of you."

Margaret patted her hand. "We're the lucky ones, Rosie. You've given us more than you know."

That evening, after the café had closed, Rosie sat on the beach with Sam, their hands intertwined as they watched the sun dip below the horizon.

"It's hard to believe how much has changed," Rosie said softly.

Sam looked at her, his expression tender. "You've come so far, Rosie. You've built something incredible here."

Rosie smiled, her heart swelling with gratitude. "It hasn't always been easy, but it's been worth it. For the first time in a long time, I feel...at peace."

Sam squeezed her hand. "You've earned it."

As they sat together, Rosie reflected on the journey that had brought her to this moment. She thought of Tom, whose love had given her the foundation to rebuild her life; of Aunt May, whose vision had sparked this new chapter; and of her children, whose unwavering support had carried her through the hardest times.

She felt a deep sense of fulfilment, not just in what she had achieved, but in the relationships she had nurtured and the life she had created.

The following weekend, the café hosted a special celebration to mark its one-year anniversary. The courtyard was strung with fairy lights, and tables were laden with an array of Rosie's best bakes. The entire town seemed to have turned out for the occasion, filling the space with laughter and cheer.

Rosie stood near the counter, watching as Emily and Peter chatted with Margaret, and Chloe served coffee to a group of tourists. Sam was helping Owen hang a banner that read, "*Thank You, St. Ives!*"

As she looked around, Rosie felt a wave of emotion. This wasn't just a café, it was a home, a place where people came together to celebrate, connect, and share their lives.

Embracing the Future

LATER THAT EVENING, after the last guests had left and the café was quiet once more, Rosie sat at one of the tables, gazing out at the twinkling lights of the harbour.

Sam joined her, setting down two glasses of wine.

"To Rosie's Café," he said, raising his glass.

"To May's Haven," Rosie replied, smiling. "And to all the people who made it what it is today."

As they clinked glasses, Rosie felt a deep sense of contentment. She had found her place, her purpose, and her happiness, not by clinging to the past, but by embracing the possibilities of the present.

Her journey was far from over, but for the first time, Rosie felt ready to face whatever lay ahead.

And as she leaned back in her chair, the sound of the waves in the distance, she knew one thing for certain: this was only the beginning.

The End

About The Author

Darryl, is a versatile author whose work spans various genres, including fiction, non-fiction, and poetry. With a keen eye for detail and a deep understanding of human emotions, Martel's writings often explore themes such as identity, resilience, and the intricacies of personal relationships.

His storytelling is marked by rich, vivid descriptions and well-drawn characters that resonate with readers. Beyond his literary pursuits, Martel is also an avid traveler and cultural enthusiast, experiences that frequently influence and enrich his narrative style. Come along for the journey.

ROSIE'S CAFE
ROSIE'S CAFE
ROSE'S CAFE
CAFÉ

www.ingramcontent.com/pod-product-compliance
Lightning Source LLC
Chambersburg PA
CBHW031800150726

47989CB00006B/2814